Bodge
Plants a Seed

SIMON SMITH

Marshall Pickering
An Imprint of HarperCollins*Publishers*

BASED ON THE PARABLE OF THE SOWER, MATTHEW 13

Marshall Pickering is an Imprint of
HarperCollins*Religious*
Part of HarperCollins*Publishers*
77–85 Fulham Palace Road, London W6 8JB

First published in Great Britain in 1999 by Marshall Pickering

1 3 5 7 9 10 8 6 4 2

Simon Smith asserts the moral right to be
identified as the author and illustrator of this work

A catalogue record for this book is
available from the British Library

ISBN 0 551 03208 1

Printed in Hong Kong

FOR ELLIE AND ED

Down at the bottom of
a long-forgotten garden
four mice were walking.

Each of the
mice had a
seed to plant.

'I'll plant my seed later,' said Stumpy. 'First I want to play!'

Stumpy dropped his seed
on the path, and he
didn't even notice.

He was too busy playing
chasing games with the squirrels.

'I'll plant my seed now,' said Big Al.

But he didn't choose a
good place. The ground
was dry and rocky.
It was a shady spot.
Big Al's seed
didn't grow.

Then the
insects came
to chew
holes in all
the leaves.

But Bodge
scared them
away.

Weeds began to grow up all around.
Bodge pulled them up and threw
them away.

And Bodge's plant grew … and grew … and grew into a big, tall plant.

Bodge took care of his plant.

It got just enough rain ...

And just enough sun …

And a big
stick to
grow up.

And Bodge's plant grew a big, beautiful flower at the top.

Stumpy, Big Al and Fat Jim
looked up at Bodge's plant.

'I wish my seed
had grown up so
tall,' said Big Al.

'I wish my
seed had
grown up so
well,' said
Stumpy.

'I wish my
seed had
grown up so
beautiful,'
said Fat Jim.

So Bodge gave them each a seed from his great big plant. 'Maybe you'll give your seed a little more care this time,' he said.

'A jungle would be safer,' he said to Snowtop,
and they made one from two apple trees, the pole that
propped up the clothes-line and three sunflowers - for lions.

Then they were monkeys hanging from the pole.
The clothes-line sagged a bit.

A few minutes later Peter came into the jungle. He looked at Snowtop and he didn't say anything, but when the lions attacked, Peter turned into a monkey too. Simon rescued Snowtop by wrestling with two lions at once. Peter wrestled with his own lion.

The lions were too fierce for
Simon and Peter.
'To the beach! To the beach!'
cried Simon. He tied his jumper
round his head and turned into
a pirate.

Luckily the haunted castle had a window open because Gran liked fresh air in her bedroom. Peter boosted Simon over the window-sill and flung Snowtop after. Then he climbed in himself.

There was a dressing-table in the castle
loaded with equipment useful for turning
people into vampires.
Snowtop grew fangs
that glittered like diamonds.
Simon and Peter dripped
lipstick blood.
They drew black stitches
on their heads and
turned their noses blue.

But suddenly . . .

Jeremy was a happy little monkey. From
the minute he jumped out of bed, every day
was one big game.

Brushing his teeth . . .

COLD!

taking a shower . . .

and eating his breakfast . . .
everything was brilliant
fun! Jeremy hopped,
flipped, laughed and
skipped all through
the day.

Today Jeremy was very excited. It was the school FUN DAY! There would be stalls and races and games and competitions all day long.

Jeremy had never won a prize before. He wanted to show he was the best at something. Today Jeremy wanted to win!

"I can't wait," he said to his mum, as they drove to school. "I'm going to have a go at everything!"

The first event of the day was the egg and spoon race. Jeremy lined up at the start with all his friends.

"Oh good," thought Jeremy, "Charlie Cheetah's not in this race. I'm sure I can win now!"

"On your marks," shouted the teacher. "Get set . . ."

Annie the Antelope bolted away so fast, her egg flew off her spoon!

Ronnie the Rhino got cross-eyed from watching his egg and ended up going round and round in circles!

Jeremy was in the lead . . . but Gilly Giraffe just beat him by a long neck!

"Well done, Jeremy!" puffed Tommy Tortoise, trailing in last. "You came second!" "I'll win the next one," said Jeremy.

Then something unbelievable happened!
Charlie had a piece of string from the
three-legged race wrapped round his ankle.
He got tangled, tripped and fell . . .

Look out,
Charlie!

. . . Jeremy was in the lead!
Charlie jumped up and ran after him.
It was neck and neck, but . . .

. . . Jeremy reached the tape first.
HE HAD WON!
"I've never come second before,"
said Charlie.

"I only won because you tripped," said Jeremy.
"You still won," said Charlie.

"Remember," said the teacher, "it's not the winning but the taking part that counts."
"You're right," said Jeremy, grinning.

"But I still beat a cheetah!"

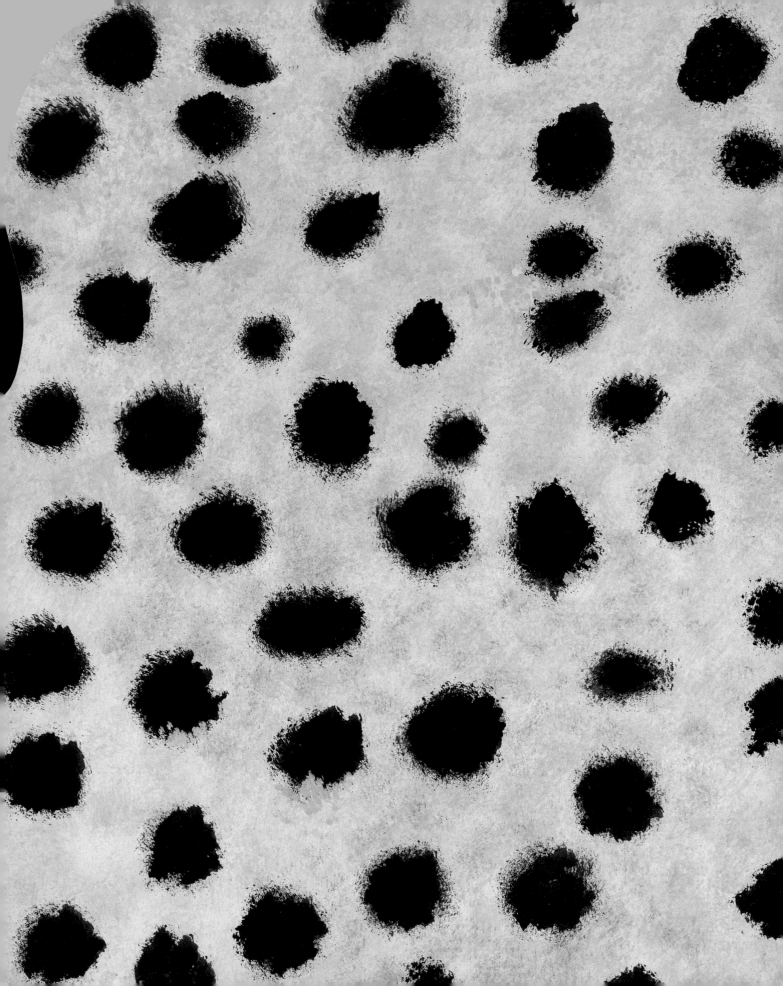

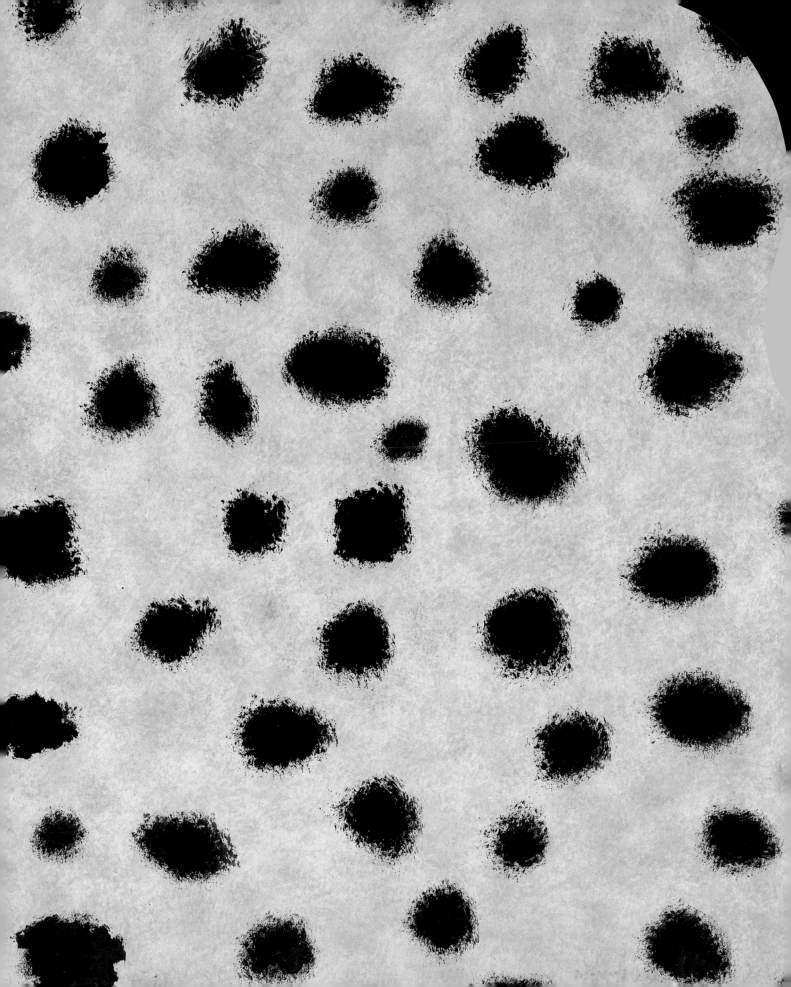